The Wheelie Thing

First published in 2012
by Wayland

Text copyright © Tom Easton 2012
Illustration copyright © Woody Fox 2012

Wayland
338 Euston Road
London NW1 3BH

Wayland Australia
Level 17/207 Kent Street
Sydney, NSW 2000

Series Editor: Louise John
Series design: D. R. ink
Design: Lisa Peacock
Consultant: Shirley Bickler

A CIP catalogue record for this book is available from the British Library.

ISBN 9780750268622

Printed in China

Wayland is a division of Hachette Children's Books,
an Hachette UK company
www.hachette.co.uk

The Wheelie Thing

Written by Tom Easton
Illustrated by Woody Fox

WAYLAND

Zip, Blob, Polly and Luna were doing their exercises.

Luna Lampfish liked to do starfish jumps. Every time she landed, her light flashed!

Just then, the clam phone rang.
"Oof!" Blob puffed. "Hello?"

It was Ozzy Octopus. "We've found something funny," Ozzy said. "Come and see."

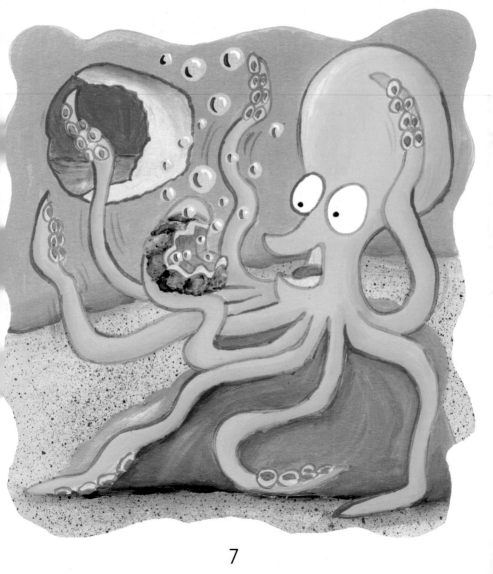

Sea Force Four raced to Ozzy's house. Ozzy and Otto, his son, were waiting for them.

"Here it is," Ozzy said. He showed them a funny thing with two big wheels on a metal frame.

9

"What is it?" Zip Marlin asked. "I think it's called a bike," said clever Polly Porpoise.

"Show them what it does, Otto!"
said Ozzy.

11

Otto sat on the bike. He used four of his tentacles to hold the handlebars. He used the the other tentacles to turn the pedals.

Otto shot off across the seabed.

"Wow!" said Zip. "That's really cool!"

"It looks fun," Polly said, "and bikes can be useful, too!"

Suddenly, the front wheel of the bike hit a rock. Otto landed with a crash in a pile of coral.

"Oh no!" Ozzy cried, and went to help his son.

"This bike is fun," said Ozzy, "but it's also dangerous!"

"Yes, I can see that," Polly nodded. "Don't worry. We'll take the bike away and we'll think about how to use it."

"How are we going to get it back to base?" Blob asked. "It looks heavy!"
"Hmm," said Polly. "We will ride it very slowly and very carefully."

Blob and Zip pushed one pedal each. Polly turned the handlebars and Luna sat in the basket.

"This is fun," laughed Luna.
"Go faster!"
"Is that a good idea?" Polly asked.

"Oh, come on!" Blob said.

So Zip and Blob pushed the pedals harder and the Wheelie Thing went faster.

"Yippee!" cried Blob. Even Polly was starting to have fun.

"Stop!" Luna shouted, suddenly. "Ship ahead!"

But it was too late! Sea Force Four hit the old ship and crashed into the side.

"Are you all ok?" Polly shouted.

Zip had shot through the air and
he had his nose stuck in the deck.
Luna was tangled up in the basket,
and her light went on and off.

Polly helped them both to get free.
"Where's Blob?" Zip asked.

They heard a groan coming from inside a sea chest. Zip sped over and opened the lid.

Blob looked up at him sadly.
"I have a sore head," he said.

"We must get rid of this bike once and for all," said Zip. "It's too dangerous."

"Yes!" said Blob, and Luna nodded her head.

"I have an idea," Polly said, rubbing her chin. "I wonder if we can take the wheel off?"

"Now we have a safe way to exercise," Polly said. "Pedal faster!"

"Hey, Blob," Zip puffed. "Why aren't we moving?"

"Oh Zip," said Blob. "I'll tell you later!"

START READING is a series of highly enjoyable books for beginner readers. The books have been carefully graded to match the Book Bands widely used in schools. This enables readers to be sure they choose books that match their own reading ability.

Look out for the Band colour on the book in our Start Reading logo.

The Bands are:

- Pink Band 1
- Red Band 2
- Yellow Band 3
- Blue Band 4
- Green Band 5
- Orange Band 6
- Turquoise Band 7
- Purple Band 8
- Gold Band 9

START READING books can be read independently or shared with an adult. They promote the enjoyment of reading through satisfying stories supported by fun illustrations.

Tom Easton is an experienced author of children's books, including lots of funny Start Reading books about the Poor Pirates! He lives with his family in Surrey.

Woody Fox has been illustrating children's books for 18 years! He was born in London, but now lives in a cute thatched cottage in the middle of Devon with his 2 cats. When he's not drawing, he likes to do mosaics, basket weaving and go for long walks!